Ida grace and the jewel of mysteries

"A Sparkling Adventure Awaits!"

AAFREEN FATHIMA R

BlueRose ONE
Stories Matter
New Delhi • London

BLUEROSE PUBLISHERS
India | U.K.

For permissions requests or inquiries regarding this publication, please contact:

BLUEROSE PUBLISHERS
www.BlueRoseONE.com
info@bluerosepublishers.com
+91 8882 898 898
+4407342408967

ISBN: 978-93-5819-401-2

Cover design: Muskan Sachdeva

Typesetting: Namrata Saini

First Edition: January 2024

Live it while you read it

The story starts with twelve-year-old kids named Emily, Ida, and Zee. One day by accident they each get a wish in which one of them 's wish comes true in a terrible way, to undo the wish, they had to go to the city of forever lost. Where they were trapped in their own thoughts, struggled to find their way out, solved mysteries, fought against gravity, and faced their greatest fears:

"Once You Enter The Forest Of Darkness,

You Can't Turn Back Due To The Forest's Starkness.

If You Focus In What You Seek,

The Forest Will Show You The Lead.

But.. **Only One Can Go Further,**

After You Face The Greatest Fear."

Who will be the one to go further ?

Who will be lost in the forests forever ?

What was the wish ?

And how will they save the day ?

Read more to find out...

Contents

Chapter One

The Mystery of the Glowing Box

This story takes place in Calonia. Calonia is one of the most beautiful and oldest cities on earth just like Linaria.

Mr. and Mrs. Grace are the parents of Ida and her elder sister Christina.

Ida is a beautiful girl with cute pink cheeks. She has brown hairs, and beautiful almond-coloured eyes.

Ida's family "The Grace" lived in the city of Calonia with her grandmother till Ida was a year old, then later Ida's family had to move to Linaria for better working conditions. Linaria is the neighbouring city of Calonia.

After eleven years Ida's parents finally decided to move back to Calonia as Ida's grandmother lived there alone, Ida was very eager to go back to Calonia and meet her grandmother, as she has heard a lot about all the amazing adventures she has been to.

In Linaria Ida made a best friend named Vincy, she liked her a lot, so she wasn't willing to leave her best friend and move to another place, Ida's parents were very happy that they were finally moving back to Calonia.

Ida knew it would be hard to adjust in a new place but she still agreed to move back just to make her parents feel better.

After moving back to Calonia, Ida just pretended to be happy.

It took more than two months to set up everything in their old house.

As days passed Ida was feeling much better in Calonia but still, it was hard adjusting to a new place especially when you had lived in the same place from the time you know.

Ida joined a school in Calonia at the end of the academic year before the summer holidays, where she made two new friends named Emily and Zee.

Mr. and Mrs. Florin are the parents of Emily and her ten-year-old brother Zack.

Emily loves her family, but one thing that annoys her the most, is her brother taking advantage of being the youngest in the family and how her parents support him in everything, even when he is wrong.

Emily is a fair girl with red hair and blue eyes. Emily is always well dressed and loaded with heavy cosmetics. Although she is naturally beautiful, she still has a craze of applying heavy makeup.

If there is one thing you should know about Emily is, that she loves to talk all the time, her pockets are always filled with chocolates and candies.

She always writes her name in all of her chocolates, candies, and even on the fruits to identify her's.

Last but not the least she also carries three pocket mirrors with her wherever she goes.

Mr. and Mrs. Miller are Zee's parents. Zee is the only child in the family which is one of the reasons he is adored by his parents.

Zee's parents love him so much that they treat him as a prince and provide him everything, even before he could wish for it and they are the kind of parents whom Emily wishes for.

Zee is a kid with black hair, black eyes, pink lips and a really cute face.

Zee is a person who likes to stay quiet, he never talks to anyone in the class which is the reason he has no friends but according to him books are better than friends, which is why he likes to spend most of his time in the library.

When Ida met Emily and Zee she felt deeply connected and she no longer felt insecure about shifting to a new school, she liked Emily's creativity and Zee being very studious.

They became best friends within a week and they felt as if they knew each other for a long time.

They became friends but each of them had a different way of thinking.

Ida is good at sports, and she also loves to invent new things. She always dreams of going on amazing adventures just like her grandmother

Emily is good at creative things but she is often found wasting her time, bragging about herself, or eating something, but overall.... She is a good friend and the best company you want.

Zee is good at his studies, especially in biology no one is better than him.

Zee likes to do everything which Emily finds boring, like going to the library, reading books, sitting quietly, writing with both his hands, and many other things.

Even after they became friends, Emily and Zee are still two different characters. It was Ida who kept them connected.

She was a bit like Zee as she likes to study and go to library and also like Emily, as even she liked doing creative things, Emily and Zee were forced to be together due to Ida, though they hate each other.

And everything was going great, until one day.....

It all started one day.... the day after the last day of school, when summer holidays begun....

On the way back from school Ida and her friends decided to meet at Ida's house to plan out their summer holidays.

But as soon as Ida went back home her mother, Mrs. Grace requested Ida and her elder sister, Christina, to clean the attic and get rid of all the unwanted stuff that has been lying there for a while, so that they get space in the attic for other things.

At first, Ida's elder sister Christina agreed, to keep up the impression, then just as their mother left she turned towards Ida and requested her to do it all by herself as she knew the condition of the attic and also because she had plans with her old childhood friends.

Ida disagreed and insisted her sister to help, but she refused to do it and made excuses, when Ida's answer was still "No " her sister blackmailed her by saying that she will help her, but before starting the work, she will tell her mother how Ida used her favourite perfume for an experiment and mixed the perfume with some salt, sugar, water, lemonade and poured it on her bonsai plant hoping it will give fruits, even before knowing what kind of plant it was, of course, it wasn't a plant that gives fruits so instead of doing whatever it was supposed to do, it killed the entire bonsai plant and Ida knows if her mother hears about it she will be furious so the very next moment Ida agreed to do it all by herself.

Just when Zee and Emily arrived at Ida's house to discuss their summer holidays....

Zee: I am sorry Ida, we would have been early if someone didn't stop by the cake shop to eat and she also made me pay for it.

Emily: Hey!! I was hungry and I forgot to bring money.

Zee: Ah! Never mind... Anyways, what do you say we start with board games like chess.

Ida: I'm sorry guys, mom had asked me and Christina to clean the attic and since she escaped, I have to do it all by myself and this will take the entire day so you guys carry on, may be I'll join you tomorrow.

Emily: There's no way if you're thinking that we are going to let you do all of that by yourself, Zee and I will help you, so we can complete the work as soon as possible and continue with our holiday plans.

Zee: What!!! I am not starting my holidays with cleaning, besides I hate cleaning.

Emily: It will be fun, who knows, you might find some boring things like books up there.

Zee: Fine... but they are not boring, they are knowledgeable books with amazing facts.

Emily: It means the same besides everything sounded gross after you said knowledge.

Zee: It is a waste talking to you.

Emily: Well, it's okay Zee, besides you are the only person on Earth who I hate to talk too.

Ida: Okay. That's enough we should go up.

When they went to the attic they saw that the attic was very dusty and filled with all kinds of unwanted stuff, packed in carton boxes.

Emily was very good at cleaning as she often volunteers in gardening and other creative activities just to escape from the class and have fun especially in professor. Mendosa's classes.

Professor. Mendosa is the only teacher whom Emily hates the most because she always figures out what Emily is up-to and never excuses her to miss the classes, unlike Zee who never miss his classes other than studies, he is not good at any other activities.

Ida may not be good at cleaning but she does take part in physical activities like sports and is also good in her studies.

Emily was faster than both of them together, Ida opened a box to clean but inside the box, she saw many things that could be useful and she wasn't willing to throw them away, after seeing those things she took another carton box and shifted all the things in the other box saying it's important to her.

She was also collecting all sorts of junk which she found in the box like bottle caps, old springs which were rusted, and many others saying it could be used to invent something later.

Zee was doing nothing but standing aside covering his face with his hands but when he saw the dust in the corners, he immediately went downstairs and took his magnifying glass from his bag.

He came running to the attic hoping to see some new species of insects present in the dust with the help of a magnifying glass.

Emily was getting furious after seeing how they were working so she made them work together with her.

Emily came up with an idea that instead of working individually they should work together and start cleaning one box at a time so they will be able to complete the work within an hour or two.

When they started working in such a way everything was almost cleaned.

After a couple of hours, they saw there was only one carton box left to clean and that one carton box was in the size of ten carton boxes.

On the bottom right side corner there was a small piece of paper glued, on the paper it was written

"Eleanor"

Eleanor is the name of Ida's grandmother who lived nearby.

Ida was very eager to know what was inside the box, but that box was completely sealed and so they had to cut the box with the help of a knife to see what was inside it.

When the box was completely cut down they saw a lot of medals and awards inside the box.

Ida was very interested to see every single one of them, because she loves her grandmother more than anyone or anything in the whole world, but due to her parent's work they were away from her grandmother for eleven years but the reason Ida wanted to see everything, is that her grandmother was a very adventurous lady when she was young.

She is still very good at sports. Ida wishes to be just like her when she grows up, her grandmother even got an award for being the bravest lady of all time.

While seeing all those medals, certificates, and awards they realised that along with her grandmother's things, they also saw a small square-shaped wooden vintage box wrapped in a red cloth.

The cloth was as thick as a block of wood, and the box looked thousands of years old.

The vintage box had cute small flowers carved on the it. five flowers, one in each corner and one in the centre.

They tried opening the box without removing the red cloth but they felt like that box was impossible to open, after a while they noticed that the box had a small keyhole in a corner which was barely visible and they thought that a key which is that small wouldn't possibly exist.

They even searched for a small key in the big carton box but they found no such key which would be small enough to match the keyhole.

Before they could remove the vintage box from the thick red cloth Mrs. Grace called them downstairs to eat some snacks Emily and Zee went down as they were starving.

Ida couldn't wait much longer so she removed the vintage box from the thick red cloth, but as soon as she took the box in her hands one side of the box glowed.

Ida was amused to see that and she dropped the box in the same place where she was standing and ran downstairs as fast as she could to tell Emily and Zee about it.

After listening to Ida they thought she was messing up with them but she looked petrified so they went back to the attic with her to see if everything was all right.

When they went back to the attic they saw that the vintage box was lying down on the floor, so Emily picked it up but when she picked it up another side of the box glowed, she freaked out and screamed after dropping the box, she was screaming over and over again that "the box is haunted" and hearing all those noises Mrs. Grace went to the attic and asked them.

"What is the matter, why are you screaming?"

Emily told Mrs. Grace that the wooden carved vintage box was haunted and it glowed, Mrs. Grace, assumed that they were making up stories and she smiled and picked up the wooden box and kept it on top of a carton box in the attic but the box did not glow this time so they were very confused for a while but Emily and Ida were still scared to touch it.

Zee told himself that there is no such thing as magic and he thought there would be a scientific explanation for all that is happening, for a moment he thought there was a sensor attached to it or a button that makes the box glow.

Zee bravely picked up the box and this time the third side of the box glowed.

Zee believed that the box is really haunted, but still Ida thought that it was very unusual for a box to do that.

She realised that the box glowed only when three of them touched it, nothing seemed to happen to the box when her mother Mrs. Grace touched.

Ida told them to hold the box together at the same time and when they took the box in their hands, all the sides of the box glowed.

There was a bright **DAZZLING** light coming out of the box and everything turned white for a while.

Chapter Two

The Wishes

Sometimes later the box stopped glowing, they had no idea what happened? As the big carton box in the attic belonged to Ida's grandmother, they thought of going to Ida's grandmother's house to ask her more about the box and why it glowed.

It was nearly 7:00 pm so they rushed to her grandmother's house, they took the box along with them, after reaching Ida's grandmother's house, when Ida pressed the bell, Mr. Han opened the gate.

Mr. Han was Elenor's watchman, he was so happy to see Ida when he opened the gate.

Mr. Han loved Ida a lot from the moment she was born although it did take him sometime to recognise Ida after eleven years.

When Mr. Han saw the vintage box in Ida's hand, he gave a weird smile and said that its really pretty and he hasn't seen a box like that from a very long time.

After hearing Mr. Han speak to someone Elenor opened the door and was surprised to see Ida and asked

"What are you doing here at this late hour?"

When Emily and Zee saw Elenor they were really shocked as Ida told them that Elenor was her grandmother but she looked very young for her age.

Ida told her grandmother that she had something important to ask her, Elenor called them inside and brought some tea and biscuits for them, and asked them.

"What is it Ida? ".

Ida told her grandmother how they found the wooden vintage box from the attic and how it glowed.

She also asked her if she knew more about the box and why it glowed?

Elenor told them that she didn't know much about the box but she did remember that she bought the box from a woman named Lora at the time she visited Linaria on a business trip but it never glowed as they mentioned.

Ida asked her grandmother if the box never glowed, why did she wrap it in a thick red cloth before throwing it away and why she kept it in the attic along with the unwanted things where no one could find it.

Instead of answering to Ida's question, she told them to go back home as it was getting late.

After listening to her grandmother, they assumed that maybe they would have imagined all of it and went back to their home.

A drawing competition

The next day morning everything was going normal for everyone and they almost forgot about yesterday.

Emily was in a drawing competition and this time among everyone's drawing Emily's drawing was the worst and she just wished that it would be nice if she gets the first prize.

But still she had no hope in her drawing this time, the time came when the judges were announcing the winners.

Emily wasn't in the 3rd or 2nd place now Emily completely lost her hope and she was packing her things to go back home but before leaving she wanted to know the winner so she stayed back.

The judge announced that the winner of the drawing competition was Emily Florin!!!!... Emily was so happy.

Her happiness had no boundaries... and she felt as though she was in the seventh haven.

At Zee's house

Zee wanted to go to the beach on these summer holidays but due to his parents' work, it might be a bit hard for them to go to the beach so he just wished that his parents' work should be postponed due to some reason so his parents could take him to the beach.

The next moment his mother Mrs. Miller opened the door and told him that they are going to the beach this Sunday as their work has been postponed.

Zee was thrilled and he felt like it was the best day he ever had, but still Zee was little sceptical about his wish granted in the same way he asked for.

At Ida's house

Christina went to Ida's room to borrow one of Ida's storybooks for one day as she had nothing to do and when she went to Ida's room she saw that Ida's room was completely messed up as there were books and other things lying on the floor, bay window, and even on the bed, so Christina told Ida to clean it up before mom comes.

Ida thought that Christina was dragooning her. Hence she told her to go back to her room and closed the door right before her in a rude manner.

Ida always hated the way her sister Christina treats her.

One thing that makes Ida go angry is that not just dragooning but she also treats Ida like a small first grader even in front of her friends and that makes her feel embarrassed in front of them.

And so she just wished that it would be nice if her sister would disappear so no one will boss over her or embarrass her in front of her friends.

After a while she realised that she left Afeena (the ball her father found when they went camping in the mountains) in her sister's room.

She then went to her sister Christina's room and took the ball but before going back to her room she wanted to apologise to her sister for her rude behaviour.

She saw her sister standing next to the bed, near the window, the very next moment her sister disappeared Ida was so shocked and didn't believe in what she saw, searched all over the room.

She searched near the window, under the bed but she couldn't find her anywhere.

Ida was so happy for a moment that her wish somehow came true but then she thought about how her mother (Mrs. Grace) would react if she knows about it and Ida knew that her mother would get furious.

Ida was really afraid of her mother's anger and started to shiver after imagining how her mother would react.

Ida was so scared to tell her mother about it but still, she had no other go.

And so she picked up some courage, went down and told her mother that she wished her sister to disappear and now she couldn't find her anywhere.

Mrs. Grace laughed after hearing Ida's imaginary story and said "That's a nice story!" she didn't believe in what Ida narrated.

Ida tried a lot to prove her mom that this is truth and she is not building up stories, but her mother could not accept it.

Her mother did not even remember that she had another daughter and said.

"Ida I know that you want a sister but this is not a reason for your imagination to go crazy and besides you don't have a sister or a brother".

After listening to her mother Ida was so confused and again asked her about Christina but Mrs. Grace again replied "No" and she also asked Ida who is Christina?

Now Ida started to imagine that maybe everyone might have forgotten about her elder sister Christina after listening to her mother's answer.

Ida thought that it is impossible to forget about a person just like that and so she took her phone and called Zee and Emily.

She told them to meet her at the park and Ida went to the park to tell her friends about what happened hoping that at least they would remember her sister.

When she went to the park, she noticed Emily and Zee were already in the park waiting for her and discussing their day.

Ida went and told them that she wished her sister to disappear and her wish came true.

She also told them that they have to find her sister but Ida only wanted to find her sister as no one remember her.

Also she had no idea of what had happened to her sister or where she is, still Ida hasn't realised what she has truly done.

Zee and Emily then saw each other's faces and told her how their wishes came true in the same way as they wished for .

They sat under an old oak tree in the park and thought about it for a long time.

And after half an hour Zee thought that everything was going normal until they found the old carved wooden box in the attic that belonged to Ida's grandmother and their wishes came true after the box glowed.

When Zee told this, Emily stood up and wished for a chocolate rain, but it seems like they only got one wish.

Emily regretted for using her wish in the competition, she thought of all the things that she could have asked using that one wish.

She thought of wishing a chocolate river, endless sweets, toys, a tree full of candy, being a fairy for a day, being a mermaid for one day, flying in the sky, seeing the planets, being the Queen of the world, getting everything for free and living the life of a royal.

Chapter Three

Grandma's Secret

Emily knew that Ida had the wooden box in her bag so she took the wooden box from her bag and cried for another wish but the box never glowed so she threw the box and said it's useless.

Ida was so worried for her sister since no one remembered her not even her mother.

Zee told Ida that they should go back to her grandmother's house as she never answered the question which Ida had asked her yesterday.

Zee was sure that there was some secret about the wooden box which Ida's grandmother was not revealing to them and so they went back to Elenor's house and knocked the gate.

Mr. Han again opened the gate and told them that they can go inside.

Ida's grandmother opened the door and welcomed them.

“I don't know why you never answered me yesterday when I asked you about the box, however I noticed that your face went pale and I feel that you know something about the box which you are not willing to reveal, but now you have to tell me all about the box because you might not believe me but, after the box stopped glowing, somehow each of us got a wish granted about which we had no idea. Zee wished to go to beach, Emily wished to win the first price and I wished my sister to disappear and our wishes came true but because of my wish you won’t remember anything about my sister even my mom forgot about her but I had an elder sister believe me please” said Ida.

Her grandmother forgot about her sister but still, she had an inkling that Ida was telling the truth and so she told Ida that “When I had the box a lot of strange things happened to me and that’s why I kept the wooden box in the attic with my other things and I haven’t seen it until today, even yesterday when you told me about the box I believed it but I never told you about it because I knew you will be fearful after you hear about it and I also tried taking the box from you but I wasn’t able to do that” Ida asked her grandmother to bring her sister back.

Her grandmother said that she can’t do that but the only person who knows about the box is Lora since she was the one who had handed over the box to her.

Ida told her friends that they have to find her sister and asked her grandmother, where can they find Lora.

Elenor told them that she has no idea where she can find Lora and she has no idea even if Lora is alive by now but when she met her a long time ago along with the box she also gave her a sheet of paper.

But whenever she tried to write something on the paper the letters use to magically disappear and she wasn't able to write anything on it and so she kept it somewhere safe and never took it for a long time.

But Lora once did tell her to use the paper to find her if she wants to talk to her, so it was worth a short.

She searched the entire house and after a long time, she brought a sheet of paper from a room and handed over to Ida, after getting the paper Ida and her friends went back to Ida's house.

Chapter Four

The Finding Map

After going to Ida's house Mrs. Grace asked them where they had been for a long time.

They replied that they were playing in the park and after that, they went to visit Ida's grandmother and came back to Ida's house, now they are about to go to Ida's room to discuss their holiday plans.

Mrs. Grace told them to be at Ida's room while she prepares dinner for them and she also told Emily and Zee that they can stay at their house tonight and she will inform their parents.

After going to Ida's room they opened the sheet of paper that her grandmother gave them but after opening the paper they saw there was nothing on the paper just like Ida's grandmother mentioned.

It was nothing but just a blank sheet of paper and they started to wonder why Lora gave a blank sheet of paper to Ida's grandmother and told her to use it to find her when it is fully blank.

They stared at the blank sheet of paper for at least three hours but nothing happened.

After a while Ida completely lost her patience, she stood up and kicked the paper with anger and said it is useless and she also said that

"I wish this paper would show me where Lora is."

When she told that, the paper glowed and a map appeared.

In the map, there were three locations plotted in the shape of keys.

They were confused for a while thinking that a person can't be in three places at the same time, also they were exhausted since they had a long day, so they thought of figuring it out the next day.

And when they went downstairs, Mrs. Grace had set the table for dinner.

While eating, Ida asked her father(Mr. Grace) about her grandmother's business trip to Linaria.

Mr. Grace: Is that so? Who said? I was not aware! As far as I recall your grandmother had never went to Linaria.

Ida : What? But grandma told me she went to Linaria on a business trip.

Mr. Grace : A very long time ago even before you were born we went on a family trip to Linaria and that was the first and the last time she visited Linaria.

Ida : Did she buy any vintage box from someone in Linaria.

Mr. Grace : I don't think so your grandmother looked very terrified in Linaria and when we asked her why she was so scared she replied that one of her sister was killed there but the truth was that she never had any siblings.

Ida: Why do you think she said that?

Mr. Grace: I don't know but once she dreamt about a fairy tale kingdom with candies and chocolates and she believed in it.

Emily: I wish I could visit a place like that in reality.

Ida: Maybe grandma was telling the truth.

Mrs. Grace: We don't know, but the reason we came back to Calonia is because your grandmother lived all alone, although we tried calling her to Linaria many times, but she always made lame excuses.

Ida: Dad can you tell me about Mr. Han?

Mr. Grace: Why do you want to know about Mr. Han?

Ida: Last time when I met him he gave a weird smile after looking at the vintage box in my hand.

Zee: I don't think he gave a weird smile he looked very happy seeing you after a long time.

Ida: I don't know why? but still I want to know about him.

Mr. Grace: I don't know much about Mr. Han but he is working as a gate keeper in your grandmother's house from a very long time, but he never worked for money, most of the time I saw him rejecting the money given by your grandmother. Once I even asked him the reason for not accepting the money and he replied that "your mother was an old friend of mine and a very long time ago she did something very big for me and that is the reason I am doing this job, so one day I hope I will be able to repay her back for everything she has done in the past".

Ida: Do you know what was the big help that grandma did for him?

Mr. Grace: No, although I did ask your grandmother about it and she replied that she doesn't remember having a friend like

Mr. Han in her childhood or that she did any favour to him.

As Mrs. Grace forgot about Christina she assumed that Christina's room was one of the guest rooms and so after eating Mrs. Grace gave Zee the guest room and for Emily, Christina's room so they could sleep there for the rest of the night.

Emily and Zee were sleeping as they were really tired after staring at the blank paper for three hours.

But Ida wasn't able to sleep for a long time as she had many questions in her mind.

Chapter Five

The Keys

(The Oak Tree)

The next day after eating their breakfast they went back to Ida's grandmother's house and showed her the map and asked her about the three keys which were plotted on the map.

After seeing the map, she said "I have no idea what it means but it looks like you have to find three keys and the keys are in the location shown on the map"

"Then what?" asked Zee, Elenor replied "I think the map will show you what to do but remember you have to save Christina before it's too late so you better get started but remember time gone is time forever lost, so use your time wisely."

Ida asked her grandmother if she would like to join them, but her grandmother told them that she is too old for adventures now.

And so Ida and her friends went on finding the three keys that are on the map.

After her grandmother's warning, they thought of splitting up and finding the keys.

One of the keys was in the park where they usually meet each other, the next key was in an old observatory and the last key was in the oldest library.

They asked for a clue to the map, and then the map zoomed and showed the location of the park, in the corner of the map it was written

"In the park near the tree."

Since there was only one tree in the park it was easy for them to identify the riddle then the same happened to the observatory, hear it was written

"In the room of 3D paintings find a star which is not a star"

And then comes the library, for the library it was written

"A book with no knowledge".

Emily went to the park, Ida went to the observatory, and Zee chose the library.

In the park Emily started digging holes all around the oak tree for at least two hours, but she couldn't find a key anywhere.

After a while Emily was exhausted and so she sat on a bench in the park, took some candies from her pocket and began to eat, she threw candy wrappers under the bench where she was sitting.

While throwing the wrappers she saw a small plant growing under the bench, that plant barely got some sun light and so Emily started to dig a hole near the plant so she could take the plant along with its roots and plant it in a place where it could get sun light.

When Emily tried to take the small plant with its root she saw a small piece of tile with the drawing of a crown on it.

Emily wondered what it could be but it looked pretty and so she tried to take it and failed to do so.

She gave up on the tile but when she stood up she accidentally tripped and kept one of her foot on the tile, with her pressure the tile went down and the park began to shake.

Emily fell down completely and when she raised her head, she saw cracks near the oak tree and stood up immediately.

Emily got terrified and when she looked inside the cracks she saw that the roots of the oak tree slowly opened up and a box appears from underground.

As soon as she took the box all the holes she dug got closed automatically, quickly the place turned back to normal as it was before.

Emily took the box and opened it, she thought that there would be a key inside it, but there was only a pendant inside the box when she opened it.

Emily took the pendant and hooked it in the chain she was wearing.

Chapter Six

The Keys

(The Observatory of 16 Hundreds)

Ida went to the observatory which is the oldest observatory it was made by a girl named Stephanie in 16 hundreds.

The observatory still looks the same as it was in the middle ages.

And in the entire observatory, Ida's favourite sport is the room of 3D paintings.

In the room of 3D paintings you can see every single star in the galaxy in a 3D form.

It is one of its kind and no one has been able to make an observatory like that because it is impossible to make an observatory which contain paintings of all the stars in the galaxy.

When Ida entered the room of 3D paintings she felt very relaxed and very happy, the stars were twinkling and appealing to see but not when you have a key to find.

Ida had to search for a star which was not a star, there were a lot of stars in the room more than she could ever count.

After sometime, she noticed that there was a star which wasn't a part of the painting.

It was attached to the top along with the other stars in the painting and after seeing that star she knew that it was the star which is not a star.

She took a ladder and climbed to the top of the ceiling, she then pulled that star and it appeared to be the right one.

Chapter Seven

The Keys

(The Old Library)

Zee went to one of the oldest libraries; this library was also built by Stephanie in 16 hundreds.

Zee was supposed to find a book with no knowledge so he opened every single book which was in the library but every single book had some knowledge in it.

After a while, he thought that it could be a storybook because most of the stories don't have morals or values in them and so he checked the story books but it wasn't a storybook.

He saw everywhere except for the reserved section but to enter the reserved section you should be a member or a daily customer since Zee wasn't on the list.

He went and spoke to the lady in charge but that lady was very strict and she told him to buy a membership card to enter the reserved section.

Zee had no other choice but to buy a membership card.

After going inside the reserved section he searched all the books which were there.

At the end, in a shelf there was a small secret sliding door, Zee had no idea about the secret door but accidentally he kept his hand on the small secret door and the door slided towards his right.

Inside the secret door he found a dusty old book and in the out cover of the book it was written "The ancient book of unlimited knowledge" but the funny part was that the book literally had no pages, it was a complete empty book that's when it struck Zee that the book with no knowledge had to be that one and so he bought the book from the library.

Chapter Eight

A Trip To Mount Ecato

After finding the keys they met each other at the park and now the map glowed and it showed the location of Mount Ecato.

Ida knew a lot about Mount Ecato since she often goes with her father on camping to that particular Mountain and that’s the place where she found her ball Afeena.

They went again to her grandmother’s house and showed her the map.

Her grandmother told them to sleep at her house that night and leave in the morning.

She also told them to tell their parents that they were staying at her house for the rest of the holidays so their parents won’t doubt them.

They went to their houses and told their parents that they will be staying at Ida’s grandmother's house during holidays and they came back to her grandmother’s house.

The next morning before leaving they packed all the necessary things, Ida packed as lightly as possible.

She looked ready for anything and everything as she knew a lot about camping.

Zee packed everything that could be used, but it looked like he carried the entire house.

Emily packed all of the unnecessary things and she was dressed as though she was going to a party.

She was wearing a beautiful frock with heels on her feet.

Ida told her that it will be hard to climb a mountain in that outfit but still she refused to listen to her.

Ida carried as light as possible but she had most of the things Zee had in his backpack.

As Ida knew a lot about camping she mostly prefers the outdoor things that nature has to offer.

They told goodbye to her grandmother and were heading off to Mount. Ecato it was a long journey so Emily started to talk and Zee was getting irritated by her boring talk and he started getting mad at Ida for bringing her along with them but Ida was trying to ignore him as she wanted to go with both of them without fighting but it was hard for her to do that as Zee and Emily are two different characters and Zee hate the way Emily does everything without thinking.

They fought all the way to Mount. Ecato but after reaching Mount. Ecato they had no idea where to go? or what to do?

Chapter Nine

The Gateway

The map then glowed and it showed the location of a cave in Mount. Ecato.

And so Emily, Ida, and Zee started to look for a cave in Mount. Ecato.

They searched for a very long time but they could find nothing.

After two hours of search Ida and Zee thought of asking the tourists visiting Mt. Ecato if they have seen a cave or even heard about it. Every person they asked to replied the same that there was no cave in that mountain.

Ida and Zee were now running out of ideas as they were searching for a cave that no one has seen.

But they had no other choice rather than believing in what was on the map as that was the only think that can take them to Lora.

Ida and Zee were trying so hard to get to the cave but Emily was tired and hungry, so she thought of taking a small break.

Emily kept her bag down opened it and took an orange, which had her name on it like her other fruits and candies.

While she was holding the orange in her hand, she accidentally stepped on a small ball.

While stepping on the ball she lost her balance and toppled over her bag.

The next moment when she stood up she noticed that her orange fell from her hand and she wasn't able to find it there.

And so she went a bit further where she saw a muddy and slippery area.

The tourists never go to that part of the mountain as it is always too slippery to walk but still Emily went there looking for her orange, but she couldn't find it.

Instead of looking for the cave, Emily spent her half an hour looking for her precious orange, but she still couldn't find it.

For more than an hour Emily stayed in the muddy and slippery area and scavenged for her orange.

At a certain place Emily stood short as she saw a tiny stream of fresh and clean water in the muddy area.

Though the place was very muddy still the tiny stream water was clean and fresh.

While looking at the gentle flow of the water Emily turned her head towards her right and saw an orange ball in the tiny stream.

When she had a closer look it turned out to be the orange she was looking for.

But now Emily wasn't much interested in the orange as she was very curious to know where the tiny stream was going.

And so she followed the gentle flow of water and after sometimes the muddy and slippery area came to an end.

After few minutes Emily reached a place where there were lots and lots of rocks.

Every single rock was different in size and shapes; Emily was walking backwards while she was looking at the rocks.

when all of a sudden she fell inside a hole, she tried coming up but she couldn't.

She then tried calling Ida and Zee to help her get out, but no one responded and that was the time Emily realised that she left her friends behind and now her friends might have no idea about where Emily was.

After searching the cave for a long time Ida and Zee got exhausted and they never noticed that they went to the other side of the mountain the time they were looking for the cave.

But when they were taking a break they remembered that they left Emily behind and they almost forgot about her.

So they went back to the other side of the mountain to search Emily, but they weren't able to see her anywhere.

Sometime later, they reached the place where Emily left her bag and so they took her bag and started to look nearby.

After searching for a while they came across the muddy area, but never expected that Emily would go in a muddy area.

So they planned to search her in some other place, but just then Ida noticed heel foot prints on the muddy surface and those foot prints looked fresh.

Ida knew that no one except Emily could wear heels on a camping trip.

So Ida insisted Zee to search the muddy area, when they went inside the muddy area they weren't able to walk normally as the surface was very slippery.

They followed the foot prints and after a while they came across the tiny stream and the orange in which Emily's name was written.

They now followed the tiny stream and finally came out of the muddy area.

After crossing the muddy area, they came to a place which had many rocks, and those rocks were different in size and shape.

Since the foot prints ended along with the muddy area, they now screamed saying " Emily ".

As soon as Emily heard her friend's voice she immediately replied saying " I am here please help me ".

Hearing Emily's voice Ida and Zee looked everywhere, but they could not find her, sometime later they saw Emily in a hole where she fell.

But when they tried to help Emily even Ida fell inside the hole and she realised that it was a cave from inside which was hidden by a big rock that was somehow had been moved and Emily fell inside it. Ida thought that may be it could be the cave they were looking for all the time, Ida told Zee about it.

Zee then came down and said "Emily you are a genius" Emily replied "I am? I mean I am" She had no idea why Zee gave her that compliment.

At the end of the cave, they found three holes in the shape of a book, a star, and a pendant they placed all three things in the hole but nothing happened.

Sometimes later they noticed another hole in the cave which was square in shape they got confused for a while as the map showed only three keys, but they need four keys.

Emily found a same square-shaped stone in the cave but as it was the wrong one, the hole shrunk when they tried to insert it and when they kept the stone aside the hole came back to the normal size.

They tried many other things in square shape but it wasn't the one.

Later Ida noticed that the wooden box they found in the attic was in the same shape as the hole in the cave.

They then placed the wooden box in the hole and it turns out to be the right one.

Since they already had the box the map never showed them the location of it.

After placing all four things the wall of the cave opened and they went inside.

As soon as they went inside the door closed but they got back all the four things they placed inside those holes.

Chapter Ten

The City of Forever Lost

They had no idea that the cave was a gateway to enter a beautiful land where they saw that the sky was pink there were white clouds all around the sky, a fully green land, a flowing chocolate river, trees made of unlimited candies, and many gingerbread houses.

That place looked so wonderful that they could even wish to be there forever but they had no idea where they were?

There was not even a single person to ask for help as no one lived there as far as they could see.

They were also scared to be in a place all alone when all of a sudden a boy came, who had blond hair, blue eyes, he looked thirteen to fourteen years old, he was nearly five feet tall, and most of all he looked very princely.

He came and asked them "Who are you? And what are you doing here?" He was asking questions over and over again.

Ida was doubtful, if she should tell him the reason for them being there or not.

But he was the only one who lived there as far as they could see and he could be of their help.

At first she thought to keep it a secret from him because they didn't know him, also he was a stranger and couldn't be trusted.

Next she thought of telling him everything as Emily and Zee completely left the decision on Ida but Ida was asking them to suggest something about what to do and what not to do as she always relies on her sister for even a small decision. She was missing her sister badly at that very moment.

Now Ida finally had no other option and decided to tell him everything.

Since she could not proceed further without help and as they weren't able to see anyone except for him, also because Zee and Emily told Ida that it is up to her to decide.

Ida thought that he would help them, and so slowly she started the conversation with him by saying "Hi! I am Ida and they are my friends Zee and Emily by the way, What is your name?" he replied "My name is Jasper and I am the prince of this place. What are you and your friends doing here?"

Ida told Jasper all about their adventure and how they found a wooden box and a sheet of paper that showed them the location of this place.

She told the whole story to him hoping that he would help them but she never said a word about Lora, instead she asked him about his friends.

Jasper: I have no friends.

Ida: why? Don't you feel lonely?

Jasper: sometimes.

Zee: It must be hard without any friends.

Jasper: Not much.

Emily: To be honest this place is so amazing that you don't need a bookworm friend.

Zee: I am standing next to you.

Emily: I am aware of it.

Jasper: Are you a princess?

Emily: Why, do I look like one?

Jasper: No, but you do look over dressed.

Emily: Ida, How dare he say like that?

Zee: I really love the way you make a total fool of yourself Emily.

Emily: How dare you say something like that about me Zee?

Ida: Stop! We don't have time for your ridiculous argument.

Emily: You think our argument is ridiculous, well we think that boy is ridiculous.

Zee: We?

Emily: Fine me. I think that boy is ridiculous

Ida: Stop!

Emily: I don't get it, why are we even talking to that boy? Why don't we just go to Lora?

Ida: Emily we are talking to that boy because we don't know where we are and Jasper can help us, so just for once put your anger aside.

Zee: Ida is right Emily.

Emily: Fine....

Jasper: What are you arguing about?

Zee: Nothing.

Emily: Honestly we are not used to talking to blond people with a lot of attitude.

Jasper: I am sorry what?

Zee: Nothing.

Ida: Hey Jasper why don't you tell us about this place because we have no idea about where we are.

Jasper: This is the city of forever lost.

Ida: This place is so amazing. And I don't know why I have only heard about this place in fairy tale but no one has ever seen this place in reality and why is this place not on maps?

Jasper: This place is not in your maps because you came here through the help of a gateway and gateways create a magical space in a place which people can't predict.

Ida: Oh... now I'm confused.

Jasper: I will tell you everything on the way.

Ida: But where are we even going?

Jasper: To my house, it's not far in distance.

Emily: Jasper is it ok if we play here?

Jasper: Sure.

Emily: Come let's go Zee.

Zee: But what about Ida? We can't leave her alone.

Ida: You go and have fun I'll be ok.

Zee: Are you sure about it?

Ida: Yeah.

Chapter Eleven

The Prince

In a minute or two they both reached Jasper's house and when Ida entered his house Ida found that there was no one, she was very confused because he told them that he is the prince of this place so she asked him "Jasper if you are a prince then Why are you not living in a castle?, If you don't live in a castle, how can you be a prince?"

Jasper: It is not important that you should live in a castle to be a prince besides who told you a person living in a castle is called a prince?

Ida: Most of the fairy tales tell that royals live in castles.

Jasper: Not all fairy tales are true.

Ida: The other houses we saw were made out of ginger bread. Why isn't your house made out of ginger bread?

Jasper: The place you just saw was the candy village, in the whole city of forever lost it is the only place where you can see all sorts of chocolates and candies, so not all houses here are ginger bread, it is mainly a tourists spot but to be honest the city of forever lost is so big that not even I have seen all of it.

Ida: Really? where are the other people of your kingdom? I haven't seen anyone since I came here. Was this place always like this?

Jasper: No, this place wasn't always like this, many years ago this place was filled with people who loved each other and treat each other as siblings, there was unity among people all across the city. There was a man named Vulgaris, everyone loved him but he wasn't happy with that, he wanted to be more than just a person who everyone liked, he thought that everyone should fear him and so he started to command others, when people refused to listen to his command, he trapped them and turned everyone into stones but there were few who escaped from the city of forever lost and came to your world through gateways, he then closed all the gateways. He thought he did but it is not so easy to close the gateways. Those who escaped and came to your world told their generation about the city of forever lost but as years passed people assumed it was just a fairy tale, day by day Vulgaris was getting powerful but one day a woman named Lora defeated him for good and no one has ever heard of him after that day, but some people say Vulgaris was defeated for good but I don't know how far that's true, so listen to me and leave this place as soon as possible.

Ida: I came here to find my sister and I am not leaving without her.

Jasper: I know you can't leave this place without your sister because you chose the wrong gateway to get here.

Ida: Wait, are there other gateways to come here? I thought that the cave in Mount Ecato is the only gateway.

Jasper: No, there are ninety-nine gateways to come here, some gateways are even inside the city of forever lost and those gateways can even take you back in time, honestly I have never went through any gateway, you and your friends came from the gateway of missions. Of course it is the easiest gateway to come here but the only way for you to go back is to complete the work for which you came here so the only way for you to go back is to find your sister, but your plan sounds a bit confusing.

Ida: Jasper, in the middle you mentioned about a persson named Lora can you tell me more about her.

Jasper: Sure but why?

Ida: It's complicated.

Jasper: If you tell me, maybe I can help you.

Ida: Fine. When we first met I told you how my sister disappeared and that's the reason we came here to find Lora. According to my grandmother Lora was the one who gave the box to her, so maybe she could be the one who knows how to undo my wish and bring my sister back. Do you know where she is?

Jasper: No but I'm sure the map must know where Lora is. Can you give me the map?

Ida: Sure.

Jasper: According to the map you have to cross the upside-down imagination forest, the forest of backward, the forest of hallucinations, and the forest of darkness to find Lora, but you have to remember that finding Lora is not going to be easy because she is the Wisest woman of all time. You might even lose something you love the most if you want to get to Lora by crossing those four forests is not going to be so easy because no one has ever gone into those forests especially in the forest of darkness and those who have gone have never returned back. I have no idea what's going to happen so it's better if you don't go, listen to me I know a way to send you and your friends back but it is your choice because this is not going to work, not just your sister but you might also lose your friends. I have no idea whether you will return safely, still it's up to you to decide whether you want to lose your sister and your friends or you want to be happy with your friends and forget about your sister, so what do you want to do?

Ida: I think I will save my sister and my friends too... no matter what happens, I will do anything to save my sister. Thank you for everything you did for me and my friends... Jasper.

Jasper: Good luck! I wish you save your sister.

Ida: Thanks. I think I will be needing it.

After a while, Emily and Zee came searching for Ida they told her that they saw a mountain of Ferrero Rocher chocolate which never ends and they also saw a garden but in that garden, instead of grass there were candies and in a particular area, they also saw giant lollipops, after listening to them Ida told them that they have to cross four forests to find Lora and she also asked them if they really want to help her even if it's not going to be easy, after all it is her sister and her problem.

Without thinking even for a moment, Emily and Zee told her that they will help her no matter whatever happens.

Chapter Twelve

The Upside-Down Imagination Forest

They followed the map and after some time they saw a board with a riddle on it.

"To enter the upside-down imagination forest just take a step or two and soon you will see from a new point of View".

They had no idea what the riddle meant but they didn't have time to think.

So they entered the forest without thinking so much and soon they realised that they were standing upside-down, there was a land up and down but the way to cross the forest was down and they were standing up and even the gravitational force was up in the upside down imagination forest so it was very difficult for them to go down.

They tried jumping, rolling, and every possible way to go down but everything was in vain. They sat together and thought for a while that why is this place known as "The upside-down imagination forest" and what did the riddle meant. Ida and Zee were thinking about it when Emily got hungry so she wished for a cake and her wish came true and when she offered some to Ida and Zee they asked her where she got the cake from and Emily told them that she simply wished for it and her wish came true then after listening to Emily, Ida wished for the gate to come up but that didn't go so well.

Zee wished for the gravitational force to go down even that didn't go right, then Ida wished for a paper and pen which she got it immediately. She then started to calculate the area and distance and wished for three strong balloons, they sat on it and then she burst the balloons with the help of a magical pin, since her calculation was right those balloons took them straight out of the forest, after all it was a thrilling ride and they enjoyed it.

Chapter Thirteen

The Forest of Back - Wards

They felt so happy that they finally crossed a forest but they knew that they had three more forests to cross and so they began to proceed.

They followed the map which took them to a place where they saw another board with another riddle on it.

“To cross this forest,
You should be honest.
You can’t go through in just a blink,
So change the way you think.”

They thought about the riddle again and again but they were only wasting their time.

Sometime later when they saw the board and touched it, the board turned and on the other side of the board, it was written.

“sdraw-kacb fo tserof eht ot emocleW”.

Those words were twisted and so they weren’t able to understand, also they didn’t want to waste their time any longer. They tried to enter the forest but the forest pushed them back, from getting inside, they tried hopping, jumping, holding hands, closing their eyes but nothing seems to work. They now started to wonder about the twisted words.

Ida and Zee started to jumble the words to make it a proper sentence meanwhile Emily wanted to see how she looked and so she took one of her pocket mirrors and started to admire her beauty that's when she saw that the board was behind her and when she looked at those twisted words in her mirror she saw that those words actually meant.

"Welcome to the forest of back-wards".

And so Emily told that to her friends. They were so happy and appreciated her. Emily was feeling very proud.

Soon they realised that even after knowing what the twisted words mean, it wasn't much useful to them. Ida and Zee began to solve the riddle while Emily was hungry again so she took an apple from her bag but before eating, the apple fell from her hand and went inside the forest but it came back in the same way as it went.

Emily now started to wonder that even they came back in the same way as they went. She thought for a while. She started relating the comeback of apple with the twisted words and after joining all the plots together it made sense.

Emily came up with an idea that since this is the forest of back-wards maybe instead of walking forward they have to walk back-wards and when she tried that it worked, now Ida and Zee had some hope of crossing this forest too.

It wasn't easy to walk back-ward, they were getting confused and most of the time they were crashing with each other but still it was fun and somehow they made it through the forest.

Chapter Fourteen

The Forest of Hallucinations

Now after crossing the forest of back-wards, they felt as though a big task was completed but they knew that their happiness wasn't going to last long, 'cos as per the map, they still had two more forests to cross but they were very hungry and thirsty.

On their way they saw a flowing river and near the river there was a single tree with multiple sweets and candies on it, as soon as they saw that they ran towards the tree and the river.

Emily and Zee ate all sorts of sweets and candies which were on the tree but Ida drank only the water from the river as she wasn't hungry and she also stored some in her bottle for later, now after eating and drinking they started to walk again, this time on the board it was written.

"The forest of hallucinations"

(The riddle was)

"Exactly what it sounds like"

They were really confused because the last two riddles weren't easy and it wasn't easy to enter either.

They thought that this one would be easy but they never knew that if they stayed there more than two hours they would be lost there forever.

Everything looked the same even after entering the forest, but after some time everyone started to see the things they wanted the most.

It was like they were in a sweet dream and they could be lost there forever. They actually went in to a dream.. Yes! they all slept!

Ida's wasn't the sweetest dream which she wanted to see, in her dream she saw that she was playing happily with her sister when all-of-a-sudden her sister disappeared and everyone were blaming her for everything.

She felt so miserable and everything turned black and when she opened her eyes she realised that it was the forest which was trying to trap her in a dream.

She opened the map, and she saw there was a big clock which showed her that she was left with only one hour and she remembered that before opening her eyes when everything turned black she heard her sister's voice telling her.

"Ida you have to go back to reality, all this is a trap if you and your friends don't cross this forest in two hours you all will be trapped here forever. Go ! Leave now”.

She realised that it wasn’t just a dream but her sister was warning her about the trap and she also realised that she was separated from her friends and she barely had an hour to search them.

She searched Emily and Zee for 45 minutes and then she found them but they were trapped inside a bubble.

Sooner the time passed the harder it got for her to burst the bubble.

Ida had the pin that they used to pop the balloons in the upside down imagination forest and with the help of that pin she was able to burst the bubble.

But Emily and Zee were still trapped in their own sweet dreams.

Ida somehow made them realise that it was just a dream and she forced them to come to reality after Emily and Zee woke up they were left with only 5 minutes.

They also had to find their way out of the forest and so they opened the map and asked for the way out of it.

When the map showed them the way out of the forest they followed the map and ran as fast as they could.

Emily wasn't good in running and neither was Zee, although he tried as much as he could but still wasn't able to run fast.

But when Emily came to know that if she doesn't make it on time she would get trapped in the forest forever, she ran even faster than Ida at that very moment and they made it just on time before the forest was locked completely.

Now, they had only one forest to cross which is the forest of darkness.

Chapter Fifteen

The Forest of Darkness

When they went near the forest of darkness they saw that all the leaves of the trees were black in colour; it felt like all the love and happiness had vanished. It was very creepy.

There was a board in front of them with no name of the forest but with a riddle on it.

"Once You Enter The Forest Of Darkness,

You Can't Turn Back Due To The Forest's Starkness.

If You Focus In What You Seek,

The Forest Will Show You The Lead.

But... **Only One Can Go Further,**

After You Face The Greatest Fear. "

After reading the riddle they were really scared, because according to the riddle only one will be able to cross the forest and they had no idea what will happen to the rest of the two or what fears they were going to face inside the forest, still they had to go because this was the only way to get to Lora.

So, they bravely entered the forest. Once they entered the forest the way from where they entered the forest was closed and they weren't able to go back so they started to walk and after half-an-hour of walking all-of-a-sudden a quicksand opened up and Emily was trapped.

Zee and Ida had nothing to pull her out, the only way to save her was to step inside the quicksand and pull her.

Ida was about to step inside the quicksand but Emily stopped her and she was screaming to "Leave" over and over again, now Emily completely sunk inside and the quicksand and disappeared.

Ida and Zee felt very sad & scared after seeing what happened to Emily, they cried, screamed calling Emily, now they had no idea what would happen next or who was next?

After going half the way with-in-a-blink tree vines started to grab Zee's hands and legs.

Zee was trying to free himself but those vines were pulling him inside.

Ida took a branch and tried to save him but those vines tried to grab her too so Zee pushed her away and told her.

“Ida you have to leave now, the one person who will go further is you and I know you will save me and Emily, go Ida go”

When the vines pulled him inside them, Ida was completely shaken for what happened to her friends.

She was left alone, scared and lost her confidence, but still she had no choice, so she began to walk.

After a while it was getting darker. There was a cave nearby so she thought of staying there for the rest of the night.

She started to set up a campfire and sat next to it, Ida felt so vulnerable and with a heavy heart she started to blame herself for everything her eyes were pouring, that was the movement when Ida truly understood the feeling of losing her sister and deep down in her heart she really regretted for wishing like that.

She told herself that her sister disappeared because of her, she lost Emily and Zee only because she never listened to Jasper’s warning and she was crying, soon she heard a sound.

“It’s not your fault,”

When Ida heard the voice she looked everywhere but found no one so she thought that after a long day she got exhausted and hence she was hearing things, then she heard the sound again.

"You are not hearing things".

Ida was shocked as the sound was coming from her backpack when she opened her bag a small green bouncing ball came out and said.

"Hi Ida"

(Ida replied)

"Afeena?".

That ball turned into a beautiful girl, Ida was speechless after seeing her, Afeena then told Ida how she came to her.

Afeena : Don't be so scared Ida, a month ago when you and your father went camping on Mount Ecato the time you found me, you knew I was perfect for you, and you always thought I was a normal ball, but in reality, I am a magical shape shifter and one of the protectors of the gateways I can change into anything I want, and I am of your age, so I haven't discovered all of my powers yet.

Ida: So there are others like you in Mount Ecato.

Afeena: Yes, but Mount Ecato isn't the only place where all sorts of magical things grow; there are many other gateways hidden there from thousands of years and it has been the job of the protectors to make sure no one goes inside for no reason.

Ida: There are protectors even inside the city of forever lost?

Afeena: Yes, It was the protectors who informed prince Jasper about you and your friends and prince Jasper hates visitors in the city of forever lost after what happened to his family and his people.

Ida: Then why did he left us to go further if he hates visitors?

Afeena: I don't know that either.

Ida: Afeena you know I am happy now that I have someone to accompany me.

Afeena: I think we should sleep because tomorrow is going to be a long day.

So now Ida had a person who could accompany her and she forgot about Emily and Zee for a while.

The next day when Ida woke up she saw that Afeena wasn't there. She came out of the cave with the wooden box in her hand when she heard a sound near the trees, she saw a black shadowy figure and so she asked it.

"Hello, who is there, Afeena is that you ? ".

She was looking at it so she could have a clear view but that shadowy figure was trying to hypnotise her to get the wooden box from her.

Ida was moving slowly towards him when Afeena called her from the back.

"Ida... Ida are you even listening to me".

Ida suddenly woke up and when she turned back she saw that Afeena was standing behind her.

Everything was normal but she still Ida had an inkling about the forest and so she was in a hurry to leave the forest with Afeena. After a long time, they finally crossed all four forests.

Chapter Sixteen

The Woman in The Cottage

Now Ida opened the map and asked for Lora's location.

The map glowed and showed the direct way to Lora and she knew they were getting close to her.

In the middle of their way, Afeena was going on talking to Ida which reminded her of Emily and she was rushing to get to Lora to save her sister and her friends.

When they reached the place shown on the map all they saw was a very dusty old cottage with a pretty door, on the door, there were small cute flowers carved on the borders, and on the top right-hand side corner of the door, there was a carving of a small fairy who was pointing her wand down when Ida knocked the door the carved fairy was talking to her.

The fairy was able to move where ever she wanted in the door, she asked her who did she want to meet? Ida replied

"I would like to meet Lora ".

When she said that, the door opened and a lady came out, the woman in the cottage was dressed very simple, she wore a single bangle in both hands, a thin gold chain with a small pendant in her neck, her hairs were blond in colour, her eyes were blue and her dress was even less than ordinary but still her appearance demanded respect.

The lady said

"I am Lora, how can I help you?".

Ida was shocked when the lady told her that she is Lora, Ida was bit disappointed, as she imagined Lora to be more majestic.

Lora invited them inside her cottage.

When they went inside the cottage it turned out to be a luxurious castle from inside.

Lora took a rotten apple and began to cut it, the apple looked years old but when Lora gave it a cut the apple looked very fresh from inside.

She offered them the rotten apples and forced them to eat.

When Ida took a bite she realised that those rotten apples were juicy and tasty.

Ida ate all of the apples as she was very hungry and she enjoyed those apples.

While eating, Ida told Lora why and how she came here, she also asked Lora to find her friends and her sister.

Lora: I am afraid I don't have the authority to do that.

Ida: But it's you, who gave the wooden box and map to my grandmother?

Lora: I never gave the box to anyone.

Ida: But my grandmother said that a woman named Lora gave the box and the map to her a long time ago.

Lora: I don't know why she told you that and I don't know how she knows me but I never had the box.

Ida: What do you mean?

Lora: That box is been lost since 14 hundreds, besides do you even know what is inside the box?

Ida: No, it's not opening, but it has a small keyhole.

Lora: What's inside the box might be the key to saving your friends and sister.

Ida: Maybe that's why the map showed me your location because you are the one who has the key to open the box and save them.

Lora: The map showed my location because you asked for that. I am sorry, I don't have the key but I am the key who knows where the key is.

Ida: What? what is inside the box?

Lora: The Jewel of mysteries.

Ida: Why is it called the Jewel of mysteries?

Lora: It is called the Jewel of mysteries because no one has ever been able to discover all of its powers. The last person who had the jewel of mysteries was Queen Aria.

Ida: Then how did my grandmother got the box?

Lora: She is the only one who can answer that question.

Ida: Lora, to find them I have to open the box and to open the box I need the key but where is the key? Please don't tell me I came here for nothing.

Lora: The key is with Kasandra.

Ida: Who is Kasandra?

Afeena: Kassandra is the fairy of justice.

Ida: Is she a real fairy?

Afeena: I don't know, I have never seen her.

Lora: Kassandra has all sorts of magical things.

Ida: Where can we find her? And Where should we go now?

Lora: She is in this castle but to get your friends and your sister, along with the key you should also win her heart. Can you do that? But I will warn you winning her heart is not going to be easy.

Ida: I will do anything for my friends, because my friends sacrificed their life for my mission, hoping I will save them, now it's my turn to save them and I can't step back.

Lora waved her hand once and a door magically appeared.

Lora: You will find Kasandra once you pass through this door. Ida, I can see you have won my heart and I can tell you how to win Kassandra.

Ida: How?

Lora: To win Kasandra you have to be true of heart because nothing is what it seems and if you believe in yourself truly more than anything or anyone you will never go astray.

Ida: Thanks.

Chapter Seventeen

The Fairy of Justice

After talking to Lora as soon as they went inside, the door closed and when they went further they found no one.

They were looking around if they could see anyone when all-of-a-sudden a fairy appeared and said

"I am Kasandra, the fairy of justice. How can I help you? "

She looked very majestic with her big beautiful wings.

Afeena and Ida assumed she was a normal lady but she turned out to be a real fairy.

Ida asked Kasandra if she could give her sister back to her.

Kasandra said "As far as I recall you were the one who wished she should disappear, didn't you?" Ida replied "I know I was the one who wished her to disappear but I had no idea it would come true."

Kasandra: Yes, but it came true. You can live your life the way you wanted, you can go back, be with your parents, with no sister to share, you can do all sorts of things you wanted, just like you wished for, Ida. Why do you want her back now?

Ida: It would be great but it is just not what I want. Life without my sister is like a world without happiness. I know we fight a lot and sometimes I do wish not to have a sister but she is everything to me and you can't take her away from me, nobody can.

Kasandra: I have seen you've learned from your mistakes but how badly do you want her?

Ida: More than anything. Lora said you are the one with the key to open this wooden box and I don't know what the jewel of mysteries does but if it can bring my sister then I want it and after I get my sister you can have it because this box has done nothing but caused disasters.

Kasandra: I wish I could keep it but there is a reason why the box glowed when you and your friends touched it. I can give you the key but not so easily.

Chapter Eighteen

The Room of Keys

When Kasandra snapped her finger, billions of keys appeared, there was a mountain of keys on the floor, walls and many keys were hanging from the ceiling she told Ida that one of them is the correct key and she will be given only one chance, which means she can pick any one key she also said that if she takes the wrong one, she will lose her friends and sister forever.

After hearing that Ida was scared because the keys were uncountable, but the chance given to her was only one, every single one was different, but they had something written on them.

Ida closed her eyes, took a deep breath and asked Kasandra

"If I choose the right key and get the jewel of mysteries will I get my friends and sister back" Kasandra replied "I don't think that the jewel of mysteries can help you to get your friends back because your sister was the only one you lost because of the jewel of mysteries but your friends were lost in the forest of darkness. I don't know what the jewel of mysteries can do, no one was ever been able to find out all its powers but I think your friends might know how to get your sister back"

Ida : How ?

Kasandra : The forest of darkness is a very terrifying place indeed but it is also a place where all the secrets are been hidden, only those who face the fears might be able to see the hidden secrets.

Ida : So, I have to save Emily and Zee on my own.

Kasandra : Yes, but we don't know what will happen if we open the box of the jewel of mysteries.

Afeena : Ida I think you should give it a try.

Ida agreed to give it a try but she still had only one chance as Kasandra was true to her words. When Ida looked up, the hanging keys looked like stars and she felt completely relaxed she saw every key but on one of the keys it was written "The key of mysteries" Afeena knew it was the one, and so she told Ida about it, Kasandra agreed that it was the right onc and so Ida picked "The key of mysteries" and yes as it was the right one Ida was able to open the box and when she took the jewel of mysteries in her hand she.....

Afeena : Where did she go ?

Chapter Nineteen

A Place Unknown

When Ida took the jewel of mysteries in her hand, she disappeared.

After sinking inside the quicksand Emily came out through water. She was surrounded by water and she had no idea how to swim.

When she saw a forest nearby she flapped her hands and legs to reach the land.

She was often drowning but still she made it to the woods safely.

After being pulled by the tree vines, Zee entered a dark room with many doors and hanging keys.

As soon as he picked a key the other keys disappeared, he tried opening a door with that key but as it was the wrong one the door did not open in fact all the doors disappeared too.

It was now a dark and empty room with no way out that's when a hole appeared and Zee fell inside it. It was a long way down.

After disappearing from the room of keys Ida found herself in a forest with no one around her except trees and birds.

She searched for help but she had no idea where she was, it was a bit scary for her to be in a forest all alone but she had no other choice rather than going further.

Chapter Twenty

The Cave of Memories

After a long way down Zee finally came out, he saw nothing but a forest in front of him, he looked very frightened and so he slowly kept one foot over the other and went further.

After reaching the forest safely Emily heard a lot of strange noises but she was very brave and she wasn't afraid of anything.

She bravely went inside the forest and after a long time she finally crossed the forest.

She was very hungry and so she searched for something to eat but found nothing.

She saw a cave in a far distance and rushed to see if she finds something to eat inside the cave but she again found nothing to eat.

The cave she entered was filled with unique and different kind of drawings, Emily loved drawings and so she touched a drawing.

As soon as she touched a particular drawing everything surrounding her changed except the drawing in which her hand was.

She saw a fainted girl near a beautiful golden flower she also saw a man standing next to the fainted girl and watching her and a woman entered that place and magically killed that man.

When Emily saw that she immediately took her hand off the drawing and everything turned back to normal.

Emily was very confused the time she saw a drawing of Christina in the cave and she came out of the cave and ran as fast as possible.

She never noticed where she was going because her eyes were closed.

Suddenly something came in front of her and she fell down, when she opened her eyes it was Zee.

It might be the first time Emily was very happy to see Zee and even Zee was also happy to see her.

Emily told Zee how happy she was to see him. Just then, even Ida came there with the help of the finding map.

Emily told Ida and Zee about the cave and she also told them about Christina's drawing but she didn't tell them anything about the fainted girl.

Ida knew that they had to go back to the cave and see where Christina was and so she told Emily to lead the way.

As Emily's eyes were closed at the time she was running, she did not remember the way back to the cave.

She was confusing Ida and Zee saying that the way to go to the cave must be after that neem tree and then she told that it must be after the mango tree, banana tree, coconut tree but finally after four hours of search they found the cave.

When they went inside the cave, the cave was filled with various drawings, Emily showed them Christina's drawing and when they touched it, everything around them changed they saw Christina in prison in a forest called "The forest of bad wishes".

Chapter Twenty One

The Forest of Bad Wishes

They didn't know much about the forest of bad wishes or where it was so they used the finding map to go to the forest of bad wishes.

After a long way of travelling they finally reached the forest of bad wishes they saw many bad wishes made by humans every day.

All the bad wishes were seen through illusions; it was more like a trial of illusions leading them to Christina.

After a while the illusions were disappeared and they saw many lockups but most of them were empty after seeing so many lockups they finally saw the one in which Christina was imprisoned.

The lockup had a lock in it but they didn't have its key, Ida was trying to break the lock but it was unbreakable.

Emily saw someone's shadow coming towards them and so they hid themselves behind a tree after seeing that shadow Emily said

"Its a giant " then Zee replied "No its a robot "

Ida : I think its a human.

Emily and Zee : Its changing shapes.

Ida : It must be one of the protectors of the forest of bad wishes.

Emily and Zee : What ?

Ida : We need Afeena.

Emily and Zee : Who is Afeena ?

Ida : I just wish I could go back to get Afeena.

Emily : Where did she go ?

Chapter Twenty Two

The Jewel of Mysteries

Afeena: Ida where had you been and how did you come back ?

Ida: I don't know ?

Kasandra: I think you did that with the help of the jewel of Mysteries.

Ida: Really ? What else can it do?

Kasandra: No one knows about its powers, that's why it is called the jewel of mysteries.

Ida: Ok, we don't have much time, come Afeena let's go.

Afeena: Go where?

Ida: Take me back to Emily and Zee.

Kasandra: Where did they go?

Emily: How did you disappear? and who is this?

Ida: I'll tell you later. Afeena I want you to distract the other protectors till we free my sister.

Afeena: On it.

While Afeena was distracting the other protectors, Emily, Ida, and Zee were trying to free Christina.

The lockup's key hole looked very familiar to Ida but still she was not sure where she saw it.

After a while Zee noticed that the key hole of the wooden box and the key hole of the lockup looked the same.

When Zee told that to Ida, Ida immediately took the key of mysteries and opened the lockup meanwhile the other protectors knew that Afeena was not a protector of the forest of bad wishes.

A protector is not supposed to leave its protecting area and come to another for no reason.

So the protectors of the forest of bad wishes thought of locking up Afeena and ask her why she came to the forest of bad wishes.

The other protectors were after Afeena and so she ran as fast as possible.

She screamed at Ida from a far distance saying that they have to leave the forest right now.

Seeing the protectors after Afeena. Emily, Ida, and Zee started to panic they told Christina to hurry up but Christina stopped to help a lady to escape along with them.

The time was running out and the protectors almost had them, Ida took the jewel of mysteries and said “Take us to the park”.

Suddenly a bright flash of light appeared and they disappeared.

When there was a bright flash of light Ida unlocked another power of the jewel of mysteries which broke all the bad wishes and curses except one.

Chapter Twenty Three

The Park

They reached the park safely Ida was so happy to see Christina and even Christina was happy to see Ida.

Emily and Zee were jumping out of happiness to see that they were still alive, Emily, Ida, and Zee were amazed that they went through so many obstacles and finally saved Christina on their own.

The lady who escaped along with Christina asked "Is this the park of Calonia ? " Ida replied "Yes ".

Lady : It has really changed a lot.

Emily : What do you mean ?

Lady : Three days ago it was different, wasn't it ?

Ida : It still looks the same to me.

Emily : Ida I think you should inform grandma Grace that we are back.

Lady : Wait Elenor Grace ?

Zee : Yes, she is Ida's grandmother. Do you know her?

Lady : Yes, she was my friend. I didn't know that she has another grand daughter.

Christina : Are you grandma's friend Alisha.

Lady : Yes.

Christina: I am her grand daughter Christina.

Lady : Christina ? weren't you three years old three days, ago ?

Ida : What's going on ?

Christina : She is grandma's friend Alisha.

Ida : The lady who disappeared fifteen years ago?.

Christina : Yes.

Lady : What fifteen years ? It felt like only three days.

Afeena : The city of forever lost is a very confusing place, You won't know what might happen next. Sometimes the time goes very slow, sometimes fast and sometimes the time would even stop. Christina spent nearly a month in the forest of bad wishes but she felt like it was only an hour.

Ida : How did you disappear Alisha ?

Lady : I remember that day, Elenor and I were taking a walk in the park where Elenor saw a lady and she helped her, in return the lady gave her an old vintage box and left. When Elenor touched the box it glowed then I don't remember why but we had a fight and Elenor wished me to disappear, the next moment when I opened my eyes I was in that forest lockup.

Christina then remembered that she had many things to do on her holiday list but she had only one day left now.

So she was rushing to go back to her house, on her way back to her house, she saw her grandmother Elenor who was also going to Christina's house as Ida messaged her that they successfully saved Christina and reached back safely.

Knowing this that Christina is back. Elenor's happiness had no boundaries. She was very proud of Ida for saving her sister after all the hardships.

She rushed towards Ida's house to meet Christina. The way seemed to be long, eyes were filled with tears, wanted to reach as fast as possible.

Finally, when she reached and saw Christina, she hugged and kissed her forehead. Christina's mother felt very strange for a while, but then she thought may be Elenor would have felt missing her grandchild.

By now, Ida's mom was as normal as before that she knew nothing about Christina's story of disappearing and coming back.

Christina was very happy too to reunite with her family, she realised soon that except Ida and her grandmother, no one knows this story of her's in her family.

Christina told her grandmother to go to the park of Calonia as Ida and her friends are there and they also have a surprise for Elenor which she would be very happy to see.

Elenor got excited and asked Christina about the surprise, but Christina responded that she would say nothing about the surprise and forced her grandmother to go to the park immediately.

Elenor then remembered that she had a book as a gift for Ida which she wanted to give her from a long time, because she forgot about it as Christina disappeared and Ida had to go to rescue her.

Now that everything was normal, she felt like it was the right time to give the book to Ida.

So she went back to her house and got the book for Ida as she knew how much Ida loves to read adventurous and fantasy books.

That book was about five princess of a fantasy kingdom called Livracia.

After getting the book, Elenor went towards the park of Calonia to meet Ida and her friends and ask them about their adventure of saving Christina.

When Elenor went to the park, she was so happy to see Ida, but just then she had a chance encounter with her old friend Alisha who disappeared fifteen years ago.

Elenor should have been happy seeing her friend fifteen years later, but as soon as she saw Alisha the smile in her face disappeared, she wide opened her eyes, she was really flabbergasted to see her and she said " Alisha? "

Elenor never believed in what she saw, for a moment she thought she was daydreaming.

Ida then told her grandmother about how they found Alisha locked up in the forest of bad wishes and how they escaped from there just in time before the protectors could catch them.

After talking to each other for a while Alisha asked Elenor that "how do you think my family would react seeing me after so many years? And what am I supposed to tell them?"

Afeena: I don't think your family would even remember that you were once disappeared.

Alisha: Really? But how?

Afeena: When Christina disappeared, no one remembered her except Emily, Ida, and Zee. Ida remembered her sister as she was the one who made the wish, Emily and Zee remembered Christina because Ida's wish had no effect on them as even they were given a wish and the box glowed when they all touched it. So I don't think that your family would remember that you disappeared for a long time.

> Alisha: Well, if that is true then I better go home and meet my family.

After Alisha left Ida asked her grandmother how Alisha disappeared as she wanted to know what her grandmother would say.

> Elenor: After I came from my business trip to Linaria, Alisha came to my house to help me unpack my bag, that day when I showed her the wooden box, the box glowed, so I got frightened and kept the box aside and told Alisha not to touch it, but she didn't listen to me and when she took the box in her hand, the box glowed and she disappeared.

After hearing Elenor's story Ida knew that her grandmother and Alisha were hiding something from them because her grandma told her that she bought the box from Lora, the time she went on a business trip to Linaria, her father told her that her grandmother never went to Linaria on a business trip but when they went on

a family trip to Linnaria her grandmother seem to be very frightened as she believed that one her sister was killed there but she never had any siblings, Alisha told them that Lora gave the box to Elenor in the park of Calonia when she helped her, Alisha then told her that Elenor wished her to disappear but Elenor told her that Alisha disappeared after touching the box. Elenor and Alisha had two different stories on how Elenor got the box and how Alisha disappeared, but one thing both of their stories had the same was Lora and the wooden box, but according to Lora she never had the box as the box was missing since 14 hundred and the last person who had the box according to Lora was queen Aria.

When Christina went back to her house everything was the same, her parents forgot that she was once disappeared.

The next day Emily, Ida, and Zee met each other in the park.

They were very happy that they survived all the five forests and also saved Christina on their own.

Ida was telling Emily and Zee more about Afeena and how she found her when all of a sudden the ground started to shake and they all fell down, Ida had no idea what she started, right in front of them they saw.....

To Be Continued....